W9-COM-946

# Tillo   by Beatrix Schären

translated by Gwen Marsh

▲ Addison-Wesley

An Addisonian Press Book

Katrin, Maya and Andrew are the three children who live in the house at the edge of the wood with their parents and their cat Mossie.

One cool evening in spring, as they were all sitting at supper, there came a knock at the door. One of the keepers from the wood stepped into the room. He was holding a tiny crumpled ball of fluff which he had found lying on the ground under the trees.

"It's a little tawny owl," said Father, "he must be about six weeks old."

"Is he still alive?" asked Katrin. "He looks half frozen."

"And there's blood here under his wing," said Father, "but perhaps we can save him."

The children found a cardboard box and lined it with newspaper. They made a nice bed for the poor little bundle of feathers.

Next morning the children were up very early.
To their surprise the baby owl looked up
at them and snapped his beak –
but so softly you could hardly hear it.
And the wound under his wing had healed.
Now they could see
that he was a proper little tawny owl.

Three days later he was
looking inquisitively all
around him and scraping and
scratching with his claws.
   What could they call him?
   Andrew wanted to call him Sebastian,
Maya thought Max would
go well with her Mossie.
   But Katrin had the best idea.
"Let's call him Tillo," she said,
and they all liked that, so Tillo he was.

Tillo was three months old now. Maya, Katrin and Andrew had fed
him on little pieces of meat and dead mice and he had grown into a handsome
young owl with beautiful glossy feathers.

"Tillo is big enough to catch his own mice now," said Father.

People brought live mice for him. But – believe it or not –
Tillo was scared when he saw them scuttling about!

Tillo was completely tame and was always surprising them
with new tricks. He would muddle up the shoes and pull out the laces with his
sharp beak. He would fly up onto the edge of the lampshade and sway wildly
to and fro. And when the postman came, Tillo fluttered onto
his cap and startled him so, he almost dropped the letters.

But there was one member of the family who had had no fun at all since Tillo came: Mossie the cat. Formerly, the children had looked after him, petted him, and played with him. Now he sat all alone in front of the house, sad and cross because of this miserable owl who couldn't even catch a mouse.

Time went by and it was high summer. Still Tillo couldn't catch mice.

"Let's try him with grasshoppers first," said Father. "Bring him into the meadow."

Then at last Tillo saw that he could look after himself. His beak snapped as quick as lightning at anything that rustled or moved.

Now Tillo had to learn to fly, too.
The children had to be careful that his sharp claws didn't hurt them,
so Andrew brought a leather glove with him.
The first flight was quite short and Tillo fluttered straight back to Andrew.

Another day, Tillo disappeared. Maya, Katrin and Andrew looked
for him everywhere. Mother and Father looked too. Suddenly, outside Andrew's
window, there was a great screeching and cawing, fluttering and beating of wings.
They all rushed to the window. Andrew was the first to see the danger
and ran out into the garden. In the branches,
right in the middle of a bush, sat Tillo with excited crows
and magpies threatening him on all sides.

Father waved his arms and
scared away the wild birds —
and Tillo learned from this adventure
that an owl should never fly
around in daylight.

Finally, Tillo did learn how to catch mice.

One night – the children were fast asleep – there was a cry
from the edge of the wood: "Tu-whit tu-whoo." Tillo became restless,
he hopped out of his box and fluttered onto the window-sill....
Next morning he was gone.
"That's as it should be," Father said. "Tillo has flown back to the woods
where he belongs. He has gone to join the great owl family there."
All the same, they were all a little sad when they saw
the empty box and looked over towards the wood.

Winter came. Had Tillo really found his family?
Katrin, Maya and Andrew plodded through the snow, spying all around them.
"Look…" cried Andrew suddenly.
They could see two tawny owls.
Perhaps one of them was Tillo?